By Meika Hashimoto
Based on the original screenplay by Elise Allen
Illustrated by Ulkutay Design Group

Special thanks to Vicki Jaeger, Monica Okazaki, Kathleen Warner, Emily Kelly, Sarah Quesenberry, Julia Phelps, Tanya Mann, Hudnut, Tiffany J. Shuttleworth, M. Elizabeth Hughes, Carla Alford, Angus Cameron, Walter P. Martishius, Tulin Ulkutay, and Ayse Ulkutay

A GOLDEN BOOK · NEW YORK

Educators and librarians, for a variety of teaching tools, visit us at www.randomhouse.com/teachers
ISBN: 978-0-375-86540-4
Printed in the United States of America
10 9 8 7 6 5 4 3 2 1

It was the opening night of a new movie starring Barbie and Raquelle! Raquelle was the first to arrive at the theater.

"Raquelle, we're so thrilled you could make it!" gushed a reporter.

Suddenly, Barbie and Ken walked down the red carpet.
The reporter left Raquelle and dashed over to the
couple. Furious that her spotlight had been stolen,
a jealous Raquelle stepped on Barbie's dress.

RIIIP!

Barbie's stylists, Carrie and Taylor, rushed to the rescue. Barbie didn't know it, but the two girls were really fairies from a secret world called Gloss Angeles. Using a little fairy magic, Taylor mended Barbie's dress. "Good as new!" she said.

Meanwhile, in Gloss Angeles, a mean fairy named
Crystal was up to no good. Crystal loved Princess
Graciella's boyfriend, Zane, and wanted him for her
own. To make Graciella forget about Zane, Crystal
tricked the princess into drinking a love potion.
It made Graciella forget about Zane—and fall in love
with Ken instead!

Back in the human world, Barbie, Ken, Carrie, and Taylor were just leaving their favorite hangout when they bumped into Raquelle. Before Barbie could confront Raquelle about her torn dress, Princess Graciella appeared with her attendants.

"You're perfect!" Graciella told Ken. "We're going to get married!" Then she and her attendants grabbed Ken and flew off!

Barbie and Raquelle couldn't believe their eyes.

Carrie and Taylor decided it was time to reveal that they were really fairies. They told Barbie that if Graciella married Ken, he would be trapped in Gloss Angeles forever.

"I have to save him!" Barbie cried.

"Ken's my friend, too," said Raquelle. "I'm coming with you."

The fairies quickly brought Barbie and Raquelle to the one wise fairy who could help—Lilianna Roxelle. Realizing that Princess Graciella was under a love spell, Lilianna gave the girls a magical mist that would break it. She then showed them a secret passage that led to the fairy world.

Once they arrived in Gloss Angeles, Barbie and
Raquelle needed wings to fly. They bought beautiful
clip-on wings and twirled in excitement. But there was
no time to waste—they had to rescue Ken!

The two girls quickly took to the skies.

"Whoa!" exclaimed Raquelle. "This is very high!"

Barbie offered to help, but Raquelle refused to let her.
"No, thanks. If you can do it, I can do it."

Suddenly, a gust of wind knocked both girls
off balance—and they started to fall!

Luckily, a herd of winged ponies swooped in and saved the girls.

Barbie knew Raquelle was a good rider. "If you lead the way, I know we can make it to the palace!" she told Raquelle.

Meanwhile, Zane had found out about Princess
Graciella's plan to marry Ken. Zane loved Graciella very
much and wanted to marry the princess himself.

"I challenge you to a duel!" Zane shouted to Ken.

Ken didn't want to duel Zane—he didn't even want to marry Graciella. Ken tried to explain everything to Zane, but Zane started throwing exploding orbs at him.

Just then, Barbie and Raquelle burst into the palace.
Before they could rescue Ken, the princess trapped them
in a magical fairy cage. Using her magic, Graciella forced
Ken to propose to her. Soon they would be married—and
Ken would be stuck in Gloss Angeles forever!

Barbie and Raquelle tried to escape from the fairy cage, but the bars were too strong.

"I'm sorry for being so mean to you," Raquelle said to Barbie. "Can you forgive me? Do you think we can be friends?"

Barbie gave Raquelle a big hug. "I think we *are* friends."

Suddenly, the fairy cage vanished. Barbie and Raquelle's friendship had transformed the cage into *real* wings of freedom for both of them!

Barbie and Raquelle quickly flew to the wedding hall to save Ken. Furious, Princess Graciella commanded her guards to stop the two girls, but Barbie and Raquelle were too fast for them.

Princess Graciella threw sparkling balls of light
at Barbie and Raquelle, but they dodged her magic.
Realizing that Barbie, Raquelle, and Ken were going to
ruin her plans, Crystal tried to grab the antidote for
the spell. Working together, the three friends kept it
out of Crystal's reach. Finally, Ken kicked the magical
mist up to Barbie.

Barbie flew above Graciella and sprayed the mist over the princess.

With the spell broken, Graciella realized she loved Zane, not Ken. Zane proposed to Graciella.

"I remember everything!" Princess Graciella exclaimed to Zane. "Yes, I will marry you."

The couple wed that very moment—with Barbie, Raquelle, Taylor, and Carrie as royal bridesmaids.

As for Crystal, Graciella had not forgotten her attendant's wicked deed. "I think doing every single bit of cleaning after the wedding reception will be a fine punishment," the princess said to Crystal.

"Thank you all for everything," Graciella told Barbie and Raquelle. "You are always welcome to come back to Gloss Angeles."

"Wait until we tell people about this place!" Raquelle said excitedly.

Princess Graciella knew she would have to work one last bit of magic to keep the fairy secret. As she transported the friends back to their own world, Graciella cast a spell on them to make them think that their magical fairy adventure was all a dream.

The next day, Carrie and Taylor said goodbye to Barbie and Ken. The two fairies flew off on their journey back to Gloss Angeles.

Raquelle arrived later and sat next to the couple. "I had the weirdest dream about a fairy world," Raquelle told Barbie. "And when I woke up, I felt like we were friends."

"That part wasn't a dream," said Barbie with a smile. "We *are* good friends."